Sarah Rochelle is a former teach
business studies. Her early inter
was strengthened by courses that were part of
her honours degree in Social Administration,
and in recent years by her marriage to the
philosopher Gerald Rochelle.

A childhood devotee of Marriott Edgar's
amusing poems including Albert and the Lion
as recited by Stanley Holloway, she began to
write poems in a similar vein about family
events. Time spent on the Fylde coast of
Lancashire and in Bradford, West Yorkshire
inspired the accent that is most appropriate to
these poems.

For this volume, no attempt has been made to
include all the philosophers that have contributed
to Western Philosophy and the introductions
concern themselves with the subjects of the poems
rather than being a stand-alone guide.

EH-UP!

Rhyme and Reason

An Alternative Guide to the History of Western Philosophy

by

Sarah Rochelle

With introductions and illustrations

by

Gerald Rochelle

Not Equal Press

Not Equal Press

www.doingphilosophy.uk

www.notequalpress.com

First published 2022

Not Equal Press

ISBN 9798801268231

For GWR, my special philosopher—beyond and within

'…and so the world runs away.'

Edward Senior

Table of Contents

Heraclitus of Ephesus (fl. c 500BC)

In the history of Western philosophy they don't come much more obscure than Heraclitus. Fragmentary and deliberately cryptic, Heraclitus means to take us beyond what we might normally accept as real. But understanding this from his work is difficult.

Only around a hundred sentences of his compact and cryptic writing have survived. From these we can conclude that he seems to have meant his writing to convey the idea that everything is connected. He sees the world as a structure made up of mind as soul and the external world. This external world is itself constructed of a 'unity of opposites'—uphill also has a downhill, the same river is different every time it is stepped into. For Heraclitus, the key to understanding the world lies in the human soul which, notwithstanding its own continually changing states, is inherently part of the structure of the external world and the continual flux of opposition and unity. He famously pointed out that stepping into a river, which is made up of running water, for a second time will never be the 'same' river as it was before—all is in flux. Amongst those who have taken him seriously in the modern world can be counted Hegel and Heidegger.

In general, his abbreviated style is difficult to approach. It is therefore to our benefit that the verses here depict his lighter, more family orientated side and so offer an opportunity to have his ideas expressed in a more easily understandable way.

A Day by the Stream with Heraclitus

Five hundred years before A.D.
There lived a man who said, 'You see,
Things are not what we think they are;
And whether near, or even far,
They flex and change, are not the same.'
And Heraclitus was his name.

It came to pass one sunny day
He took his children out to play;
'Back to the stream!' the children cried,
But Heraclitus frowned and sighed,
'I know to go back would be nice—
You can't get in the same stream twice.'

'But there it is', the children said,

'The water's cool above its bed;
We long to feel it round our toes.'
But Heraclitus scratched his nose,
'In winter yonder stream was ice;
You can't get in the same stream twice.'

The smallest child began to cry
And said, 'But, Dad, I can't see why
It was ice, now it's liquified;
And there is something else beside:
The water running past my toe
Was there, but then I watched it go!'

Their mother came upon the scene,
'Why Heraclitus, don't be mean;
Just let the kids enjoy their game—
The water's changed, the stream's the same.
I wash your robe here ev'ry week,
Unchanging water'd make it reek!'

Then Heraclitus smiled and said,
'It all comes clear, just use your head;
The bow must move against the lyre,
A flint on stone produces fire;
Each in one city has his role,
All things have parts and yet are whole.'

'I'll second that,' his wife replied,
'And all the meals that I provide
Are made of many smaller parts:
Flour into bread and fruit in tarts.

The heat of fire completes the dish—
A transformation if you wish.'

Then Heraclitus laughed and said,
'It must be time that we were fed;
The fire that changes parts to wholes
Has stoked my appetite with coals;
And what is clear to any dunce:
Each meal is eaten only once.'

Socrates (470-399 BC)

As Plato's philosophical inspiration, Socrates must be seen at the heart, indeed as the foundation, of all that became Western Philosophy. Socrates wrote nothing and his life and teaching is known only through the dialogical writings of Plato, as a caricature in Aristophanes' *Clouds*, and through Xenophon who provided an account of Socrates' trial. Unavoidably, Plato's account in some ways creates a character that represents many of Plato's own ideas while embodying the ideal philosopher misunderstood and unjustly treated. Aristotle came to study in Plato's Academy in 387 BC so would have been aware of Socrates as a living philosopher and as the interlocutor in Plato's dialogues.

Apart from military service in which he fought against the Spartans in the Peloponnesian war, Socrates spent his life in Athens. His father was a stone mason, his mother a midwife. He married Xanthippe with whom he had three children. Socrates rejected the professional approach to philosophy used by the Sophists and refused to take money for his philosophising method. This meant that practically he lived a meagre life.

Although he was critical of democracy, he was a staunch upholder of the authority of the state and its judicial system. After the brief period when power was taken by the Thirty Tyrants (404 BC), it was the restored democracy that accused him of the vague charge of corruption of the young which then led to his condemnation to death. The works of Plato that surround Socrates' trial and ultimate death are: *Apology*, a version of his defence at the trial; *Crito*, his reason for refusing to take the opportunity to escape from prison and *Phaedo*, an account of his final hours describing ideas on the philosophy of life, death and immortality, and the depiction of Socrates' death as the ideal philosophic death.

Even though it is difficult to differentiate the ideas that can be separated and attributed independently to Socrates and Plato, it seems clear that Socrates held that virtue is wisdom or knowledge and that wrong is never done willingly. He claimed that he knew nothing and was therefore always seeking truth by questioning and criticism—'elenchus'; 'examination'. This dialectic technique was, according to Plato, not, as it was in the case of the Sophists, to win arguments but instead to lead to better understanding.

Throughout the ages Socrates has remained an example of both personal and intellectual integrity which inspired, in the Hellenistic period the Cynics, the Sceptics and the Stoics, and in some way all others since.

Our verses here envisage Socrates at home, wishing for a quiet lie down on a grassy slope (which he was famed for). His daughter engages him in the kind of questioning which he used with his followers, though in her case there is an undercurrent of teenage rebellion and an anachronistic awareness of equal opportunities for women.

Socrates at Home

Said t'wife of Socrates one day
'I'm off to market, but you stay
To watch the kids—don't let them fight;
This time I hope you'll get it right!'

Her husband smiled and said he would
Teach all kids virtue if he could;
But as it was, he had no clue
Of what was counted true virtue.

His wife just sniffed and tossed her head,
'Children will follow how they're led;
You show them reasons by the score—
But they will think up plenty more.

They need to know who's boss', she said,
'So just be firm and use your head
Devising rules for them to learn,
Not arguments for them to turn.'

When she had gone, her husband found
A likely spot upon the ground;
He lay down on this grassy slope,
A peaceful day his secret hope.

But not for long! His eldest child,
A daughter, feisty, no way mild,
Discovered him, and straight away
Showed him that she had lots to say:

'Please tell me, father, if you would,
Whether you want me to be good.'
Her Pa replied, 'Of course I do;
Your brothers and your sisters too.'

'You say virtue is knowledge-based;'
Argued the girl, 'And so I'm faced
With knowing you don't care for me;
And it's unfair as you can see.

My brothers learn more every day
From tutors you are pleased to pay;
Your love and care will help them grow
In virtue, as I'm sure you know.

But what of us, the family girls?
You give us money for our curls,
And compliment us on our dress,
But this is really something less.'

Her father sighed and kissed her cheek,
'True wisdom comes to those that seek

As you do, looking into life,
Exploring it as with a knife.

But in this State we play our part;
The knowledge *you* need is the art
Of keeping house and being a wife
And that way lies *your* virtuous life.'

His daughter was not mollified,
'But what *is* virtue, Pa,' she cried,
'If first it's one thing, then another;
It's this for sister, that for brother?'

'I find I cannot answer you,'
Her father said, 'And that will do
As now it's time to make the tea
For all the family and for me!'

Plato (428-347 BC)

Together with Aristotle, Plato is the best known of all Ancient Greek philosophers. Born into a noble family but inspired by his teacher Socrates, he chose a life devoted to philosophy over what, according to his rank, would have been a life of statesmanship. Angered by the Athenian state's sentence of death on Socrates, he left Athens for many years. Upon his return he founded the Academy which provided the model for higher education thereafter.

Plato was a prolific writer. All his works, with the exception of an account of Socrates' trial in the *Apology,* are written in dialogue form. His style is elegant and philosophically penetrating. His work is generally divided into three periods. The early period is the only record we have of Socrates' dialogues and brings out Socrates' concern with virtue and its role in true knowledge. In the middle period, Plato puts into Socrates' character more of what are considered Plato's own thoughts. Here he explores his metaphysical and epistemological ideas and, in the case of the *Symposium*, with love as the background. Further, he investigates the idea of knowledge when applied to common ethical and aesthetically orientated areas of human enquiry and from this proposes the idea that the 'Forms' are the true model that lie behind all things that appear or are recalled in the world as we experience it. He looks closely at the nature of the 'soul', concluding that its immortal reasoning part passes by 'transmigration' from one life to the next according to its performance in previous lives. The world of the Forms is only ever available to the intellect and not the senses. Plato was not a democrat and believed that the state's power should be controlled by a ruling class who have proved themselves proficient in debate and have discovered for themselves the true nature of the good. He believed that members of the state should contribute fully by fulfilling their given role and abiding by the laws. His third period restates his thinking up to this point and introduces more exacting analysis of language, its parts and function, and again asserts the role of the expert as being above the law and any wishes of the members of the state.

Plato's thoughts have had enormous impact on western philosophy and Christianity. His pupil Aristotle, who set up his own school in Athens, the Lyceum, pressed on with and took further the main subjects of Plato's work: metaphysics, logic and mathematics. Thereafter, and until the present day, all areas of philosophical enquiry, if not Platonistic, are at least within the framework that Plato initially prepared. The most outstanding neoplatonists are Plotinus and Porphyry. But the influence of Plato's thought can be found in the philosophy of Bergson, Hegel and McTaggart, the poetry of Blake, Shelley and Keats, and within the ideas of Emerson and the American transcendentalists.

In our verses here we find Plato recalling Socrates' love of a perfectly sloping grassy bank upon which to lie, while at the same time not missing the chance to get in a mention of his famous allegory of the cave.

An Academic Outing

It were back in the days of the Ancients,
Round about three six seven BC—
The folk didn't like counting backwards
But were still waiting t'birth of J C.

They were planning the annual outing
At Plato's new academia;
The students were jostling and shouting
'Til Plato called out, 'Listen here!

We'll need a good place for the outing,
Some food, drink and surely some sex;
So put on your thinking caps now, lads
And help me plan what we do next.'

The choice of the place caused confusion,
They argued it out for a day
'Til Plato remembered his teacher
And asked, 'What would Socrates say?'

One bright spark said he had remembered
That Socrates favoured the grass,
But it had been quite wet around Athens
So they let that suggestion just pass.

'I fancy a cave,' said old Plato;
The students all let out a sigh,
'We want somewhere real,' they grumbled;
So Plato's idea didn't fly.

At last they agreed on a venue
That suited them all to a tee;
It was a quite small private garden—
A bit overgrown, but no fee.

'And now for the food!' someone shouted,
'We'll all bring some wine and some bread,
With olives and dates and some ouzo
There'll be plenty to get us all fed.

For sex I have had an idea,
And we're Greek so it's not queer or strange,
We have all had our fill 'o Sophia
So we'll try Rhet or Rick for a change.'

Well, the outing went off as expected,
And everyone said it were grand,
So old Plato's academia
Was voted the best in the land.

Zeno of Ilea (fl. c. 470 BC)

An associate and fellow citizen of Parmenides (*fl.c.* 480 BC) and admired by both Plato and Aristotle, Zeno of Ilea did not put forward any positive theories but instead proposed paradoxical arguments which set out to destroy the validity of ideas about things in the world commonly accepted as irrefutable.

Zeno argued that it must be possible for things to be so large as to be infinitely large and so small as to be infinitely small, and because any thing can be divided into two this must also bring about an infinite regress. Aristotle records Zeno's paradox of motion exemplified by the runner in the stadium who, before being able to run the whole length of the course must first complete one half of it and before that must first cover one half of that distance. This process is infinite and so the runner can never get to the end of the race. In a similar way, a fast runner—Achilles in his example—can never catch a slow runner to whom he gives a head start. He argues against motion saying that an arrow is at any instant of its flight motionless, and if that is the case then it cannot also be moving.

The influence in philosophy of this sort of thinking has been great—running a problem down to its basics is a sound and recognised way of analysing and challenging premises. Descartes' 'cogito ergo sum' is the result of this sort of thinking process.

In "The Academy v Lyceum Marathon 330 BC" Zeno is not featured as a main character but it would not be possible without him, and he would not have been possible without his parents, who would not have been possible without their parents, who would not have been possible without their parents, who would not...

Xenocrates (396-314 BC)

Xenocrates succeeded Speusippus as head of Plato's Academy. His work, known only through the biography by Diogenes Laertius, attempted to shape Plato's ideas into a system and respond to Aristotle's criticisms. It is to Xenocrates that we owe the important division of knowledge into philosophy, physics, ethics and logic. And in doing this he shaped much of what followed in the Hellenistic tradition.

In "The Academy v Lyceum Marathon 330BC" Xenocrates leads his Academy team against that of Aristotle's Lyceum in this competitive event.

Aristotle (384-322 BC)

As a young man of seventeen, Aristotle studied under Plato at the Academy. On Plato's death in 348/7 BC and Speusippus' succession to the headship, Aristotle left Athens for Macedonia, at one time tutoring the young Alexander. When he was forty-nine he returned to Athens and started his own school, the Lyceum. Twelve years later, upon Alexander's death in 323BC, a strong anti-Macedonian feeling in Athens brought about a charge of impiety against Aristotle. He escaped to Chalcis where, a year later, he died.

No-one has been more influential in philosophy and in some ways in the advancement of civilisation as a whole, than Aristotle. He wrote on logic, ethics, physics, metaphysics, epistemology, biology, meteorology, dynamics, mathematics, psychology, rhetoric, dialectic, aesthetics and politics. His careful, insightful and penetrating work is unmatched. His contribution to logic is enormous, with his construction of the fundamental system of deductive inference—the syllogism. He wrote on how to achieve the good life by reflectiveness and the cultivation of a virtuous character brought about by virtuous action and an understanding of the nature of virtue. Always emphasising the practice of virtue, Aristotle's plan for a good life involves the virtuous in the recognition of the good as a thing in itself as well as a personal virtue which itself allows virtue to be recognised.

Politically he took an opposing view to Plato, condemning the place of the "Guardians" and upholding democracy in which all members of the state achieve wellbeing. For Aristotle, slavery is justified as natural. Although he made much of observing the world, he did not bring about a strictly scientific method. Following his death, Aristotle was studied, discussed, elaborated upon and criticised by Athenian philosophers until the Athenian schools were closed by Justinian in 529AD.

It was not until the twelfth century AD that his work again came to light when it found its way from Syria and the Arab countries into Europe via Spain. Although study of his work was banned by the Christian Council of Paris in 1210, the discovery of many of his manuscripts in Constantinople by the Crusaders and their subsequent translation into Latin, meant a flourishing of interest that underpinned the Renaissance. St Thomas Aquinas' attempt to reconcile Christian theology with Aristotle's philosophy brought Aristotle into prime position in all matters philosophical. Although his work has been in and out of favour, he remains an inspiring influence and trigger for thinking in most areas of human concern and consideration.

In our verses here, the rivalry between Plato's Academy (now headed by Xenocrates) and Aristotle's Lyceum leads to a competitive marathon being proposed.

Aristotle's team is fitter because of their perambulatory habit while philosophising, but they become easily distracted by knotty philosophical problems and the result of the competition resembles that found in the story of Achilles and the tortoise.

The Academy v Lyceum Marathon 330 BC

In Athens of old.
As I've heard it told,
There were two schools of philosophy;
They were rivals in thought,
And they could have fought,
But did something else, as you'll see.

Xenocrates, head
Of t'Academy, said,
'Our ex-pupil's set up a Lyceum.
His name's Aristotle,
He doesn't lack bottle
If he thinks he can outsmart our team.

If Plato were here
We'd have nothing to fear;
He'd wrestle the man to the ground.
But now that he's dead
It's our job instead,

And our way to honour is found.

So who's for a run?
Come, there must be someone,
Who can hurdle or wrestle or race?'
A silence ensued
As blushes imbued
Each chubby Academy face.

'But sir, we're not real!'
Was t'pupils' appeal,
'Our Form is not universal;
A real athlete
Escapes a defeat
By regular active rehearsal.'

'It's true,' said the boss,
'We'll be at a loss
With our sedentary habits of talk;
While at the Lyceum—
You really should see 'em—
They all think and talk as they walk!'

Xenocrates then
Began chewing his pen,
And the pupils each furrowed his brow;
Until one of them said,
'We could try this instead;
I'll explain what I thought of just now:

I heard of a fable—

Recall, if you're able—
That came down from Aesop the slave.
It concerned a reptile,
Achilles, with a smile,
Said he'd race if the tortoise were brave.

You'd think Achilles won,
But he stopped to have fun,
And the tortoise toiled steadily on.
The moral's about
How persistence wins out
And that tortoise proved it no con.

Let's run a replay
Of that fateful day
When t'Greeks beat t'Persians at Marathon;
Like the soldier who ran
With the news, so we can
Have a race from there up to t'Parthenon.'

So t'challenge was sent
To t'Lyceum, and went to its chief, the great Aristotle.
He was known to be wise,
And they told us no lies
When they said he had plenty of bottle.

'See here, lads,' he said,
As he nodded his head,
'Academy mob's asked us to race.
So let's give 'em one,
And we'll have the most fun;

They're unfit and we have more pace.'

A date was agreed
And they travelled with speed
To the Marathon spot they had set.
'We'll give you a start,
As we do have some heart,'
Said t'Lyceum team when they met.

'Oh, we think we'll win,'
Said Xenoc with a grin.
'Your favours are surely misplaced.
But we'll take the let
And make you a bet
That you'll find yourselves badly outpaced.'

T'Academicians began,
And they puffed as they ran,
And could hear t'Lyceum men coming after.
Those didn't puff,
And if that weren't enough,
They were sure they could also hear laughter.

But t'Lyceum team
Said, 'Our run's a dream;
For motion is just a chimera.
Despite all our pain
We won't make a gain,
And so we can never get nearer.

When they have begun,

The distance they run
We need to run after, that's clear.
But then they've run more
And they still go before,
While we remain back in the rear.'

Ah, that's from old Zeno;
I know that it seems so
Unlikely, as we know we travel.'
Aristotle slowed down
As he said with a frown,
'It's a problem for us to unravel.'

They slowed to a walk
To continue their talk,
While t'Academy team stumbled on;
Those were now distant specks,
And when they looked next,
By Achilles and Zeus, they were gone!

Aristotle said, 'Team,
You know it would seem
That our rivals will reach Athens first;
But fear not nor fret
For, while we lose t'bet,
We gain that for which all of us thirst.

Our goal is the kind
That enriches the mind:
To live life as well as we're able,
And there's more to this race

Than a fast running pace,
As Aesop revealed in his fable.

The tortoise has won,
But did he have fun
As he plodded the length of the track?
While we will have time
Those green hills to climb,
And enjoy t'view 'ere we go back.'

So, the moral you ask?
Is, for every task,
Look for t'value in just taking part;
We don't have to win
(Though to do so's no sin);
Find fulfilment right from the start.

Epicurus (c. 341-270 BC)

Epicurus was a prolific writer who took on as a basis
for his thought the atomism of Democritus. He
established the "Garden" in Athens where friendship
and philosophising could take place in a simple, quiet,
and fulfilling environment. Much of his work survives,
recorded by Diogenes Laertius. His theory states that
the world consists of indestructible and indivisible
matter (atoms) existing in an eternal void. The aim of
life is happiness and the process of the good life that
leads to it must deal with the ever pressing obstacle of
anxiety. We must, according to Epicurus, rid ourselves
of all anxieties about god, death and pain. This done,
we can lead a life of fellowship with others where,
although nothing is barred, everything is undertaken
with a moderation that brings about complete
satisfaction. His system stands in opposition to most
Christian beliefs: it denies a benevolent god and
immortality in favour of the values of the world in
which we find ourselves.

*In "Epicurus and Zeno at the Market" we see how
Epicurus favours finding alternative paths if the one
being followed becomes unsatisfying.*

Zeno of Citium (334-262 BC)

Zeno of Citium (Zeno the Stoic) was a product of the great period of growing enlightenment in Ancient Greece. None of his writings are extant but he is attributed with having a strong belief in the empirical reality of the world, our ties to a committed moral duty, and the necessity of upholding the law and respecting the power of the state. He held an absolutist view whereby we either reach or fail to reach an understanding of the nature of things.

In "Epicurus and Zeno at the Market" we see how Zeno favours endurance as the way to deal with adversity, in contrast to Epicurus' view that a more satisfying alternative should be found.

Epicurus and Zeno at the Market

In Athens 306 BC,
Two thinkers lived as we shall see:
One, Epicurus, had a base—
His kitchen garden was the place.

The other, Zeno, worked in town;
In t'painted porch of high renown;
The Stoa Poikile—the same
That gave the Stoics name and fame.

These thinkers each had founded schools;
And while they both were far from fools,
They each professed a sep'rate creed
And to their students gave a lead.

Epicurus one day shopped
In the agora, and he stopped

To hear what Zeno had to say
On this fine, crowded market day.

A seller of amphora cried,
'How is it just, when I have tried
To serve the market ev'ry day,
An upstart steals my trade away?'

Zeno replied, 'It may seem wrong
When your advantage for so long
Has served you well, but think it through:
The buyer may want something new.

Each man must look to find his role
Within the ordered, cosmic whole;
Refrain from fighting how things are;
Enduring's the best way by far.'

Now Epicurus begged to say,
'I think there is another way:
This anxious man will stay in pain
If he sells the same goods again.

For us the world has no fixed plan;
No gods ordained when we began
That we should listen to their voice
When making individual choice.

This man's good profit from his trade
And t'reputation he has made
Both give him joy, but now they're gone

It might be time for moving on.

He can be free to live his life,
Without anxiety or strife;
Content in simple joys and diet
To live unseen in friendly quiet.'

The merchant smiled and turned away;
Packed up his stall, called it a day.
'For after all,' he said, 'it's true:
There's lots of other things to do.'

Augustine, Saint, Bishop of Hippo
354-430

Living during the formative period of early Christianity, Augustine contributed more as a philosopher than as a figure in the history of the Christian Church. He spent time in Carthage and Milan where he had opportunity to discuss and consider philosophical topics. In 388 he returned to his birthplace of Thagaste in Numidea (now Souk-Ahras, Algeria) where he set up a community of disciples and wrote, among other things, on the problems of evil. In 391 he became presbyter at Hippo (now Annaba, Algeria) and later Bishop there. From then on, although continuing as the most prolific writer, his concerns were more polemical than strictly philosophical. In his *Confessions* he frankly admits to his morally reckless past and re-commits to the Christianity into which he had been born.

His intellectual route to escaping a pagan past was formed from the Latin classical world, his Platonism being drawn from Plotinus and aimed at upholding God and Christianity against the scepticism of Cicero. Augustine's God is the creator of all things, is incorporeal and immutable. For Augustine, our senses do not provide knowledge as they are part of the decaying world. Knowledge can only come from enlightenment by God. Augustine was a dualist, believing we are a combination of body and soul, the soul somehow surviving after death until the general resurrection. On scepticism he was a precursor of Descartes, arriving at the dictum "si fallor sum"—"if I am wrong, I exist".

On the question of time, he believed God outside time and also the creator of time. Time itself, he believed, (as Aristotle had) is either past, future or duration-less; the apparent nature of it being merely a description of how we apply our measurement of it.

Augustine held that the nature of free will was the nature of choice; choice for the good being guided by God, choice for the bad being guided by self.

Augustine was mainly influenced by the depiction of the struggle between the spiritual light and the material world of darkness in Manichaeism and the reaction against the materialistic world described by Epicurus and the stoics in the form of Neo-Platonism. In his later life, however, he was driven by an unavoidable acceptance of Christianity as the religion of the Roman State and the pressures brought about by that.

Our verses here imagine Augustine arriving at the gates of Heaven on his canonisation by Pope Boniface which happened several hundred years after Augustine's death. Saint Peter and St Michael take him to task about his early immoral life and the way in which he condemned the same kind of behaviour in others after he had re-converted to Christianity.

A Heavenly Test of Calibre for the Canon

'Twere the turn of Peter, also Mike
To guard the gates of Heaven;
Pete had the keys, Michael his pike,
On shift from ten to seven.

'Eh-up, Mike', St Peter said,
'There's someone at the gate;
But if they're looking for a bed
I fear they'll have to wait.

Go take a gander who is there,
They'll have to join the queue;
We have to work by what is fair
And give each case its due.'

St Michael went down to enquire
And back again he came,
'T'chap says he comes from Hippo, sire,
Augustine is his name.'

'Who sent him?' then enquired his mate,
'It really is a cheek;
We have no rooms at basic rate:
This is the third this week!'

'He said Pope Boniface,' said Mike,
'Eight hundred years late;
That long to join the canon, like,
Seems long enough to wait.'

St Peter said, 'We'll hear his claim,
To get the thing resolved;
This job has never been the same
Since Popes have been involved.'

Mike brought Augustine through the gate,
And gave Pete back the keys;
Augustine, in a nervous state,
Was far from being at ease.

'Now, son, let us hear from you
Your claim to be a saint;
I've read t' Confessions and my view
Is really that you ain't.'

So said St Peter. Augustine

Spoke then with head hung low,
'I cannot say I'm without sin,
And this both of you know.

I womanised, drank and caroused,
But then I saw the light;
I left my mistress un-espoused
And started living right.'

'You sought forgiveness for the way
You lived,' said Mike, 'your sin;
'But look now at the part you play
In setting Church doctrine.

You tell the folk they're doing wrong
To feel lust at all;
You lay it on a bit too strong
And blame it on The Fall.

It really costs a lot of grief
And takes our time as well,
For folks' confessions are not brief
When they're afraid of hell!

I'll tell you what, we'll let you in:
You tried to do your best;
You had your fun, enjoyed your sin,
And then went and confessed.

But if you join the canon here,
You'll have to earn your keep;

The price of wings is very dear
And haloes don't come cheap.

So when a lustful mortal prays
And begs for intercession,
Your job will be, through night and day,
To hear their whole confession!'

René Descartes (1596-1650)

Descartes took philosophy out of the world of Renaissance Scholasticism into which he was born, and launched it into a new way of thinking. His work introduced the world to science and logical method which underpinned the seventeenth century enlightenment. Part of his early work proposed that all matter was essentially the same, whether it was terrestrial or celestial. This had anti-Christian implications and, written at the same time that Galileo was condemned by the Roman Church, Descartes held back on its publication. When he did bring this work out (anonymously), its discussion on the existence of God and the relation between mind and body opened up radical metaphysical and epistemological questions for a new era of philosophising.

In his *Discourse* and *Meditations* he set out to show the difference between a world rigidly described by physics and mathematics and the often unreliable world of the senses. He developed a method of doubting that led him into completely new areas: wondering about the lack of difference between waking and dreaming and even that everything we know could be a dream orchestrated by a malicious demon.

For Descartes, escape from the despair of doubt is found in the concept of infinite perfection, itself guaranteed by the existence of a perfect God. Such a

God could not possibly be a part of anything that is not itself perfect. Indeed, on this "ontological" argument (originated by St Anselm), God is by definition the total of all perfection. All existence is part of that perfection, so all existence is inseparable from God's existence. On this basis, if I can conceive of a perfect God, then a perfect God must exist; and that perfect God exists because I conceive of Him. This "Cartesian circle" is open to the criticism that if we have to prove the existence of God to validate the reliability of our own mind, it is questionable whether or not we can trust our minds' workings in the first place. But for Descartes, God is the reliable validator of all things.

Descartes is a dualist—believing the mind (or soul) is distinct from the body although both are closely and deeply intermingled. His "Cartesian dualism" in which mind and body operate together in some mysterious way, laid the ground for the still continuing philosophical discussion of the "mind-body problem".

Descartes died of pneumonia at the age of fifty-three on a visit to Sweden.

In "The Evil Demon Speaks", the "Evil Demon" which Descartes proposed as a possible malicious originator of reality, has his say. As Descartes has concluded that he himself exists because he thinks, the evil demon asserts that Descartes has created him by thinking of him.

Descartes also makes an appearance as goalkeeper in "The Enlightenment Philosophers' Seven-a-side Football Team" The other philosophers in the team rely on his ideas informing their own.

The Evil Demon speaks

'You think, therefore I am, Descartes—
Cogitas ergo sum—
But let me say right at the start,
You've got a cheek, by gum!

First off, you casually assume
I'm of the male sex;
Monsieur or mister's now my doom:
I'd rather be MX!

And second, I would like a name;
You've given lots to God;
I know that I am not the same,
But "Demon" just seems odd.

My third beef is the way you call
My acts evil and bad;
If I had any power at all
I'd call them *good*, my lad!

So lastly, let me make it clear,
Things being as they are,
You know that I am your idea
But then you go too far:

You set me up as if I can
Decide what I should do,
But if I could, Descartes, my man,
I'd not spend time on you!'

George Berkeley (1685-1753)

Berkeley lived a remarkable life. Educated at and then becoming a Fellow of Trinity College, Dublin, he was ordained in 1709. He married in 1728. Between 1728 and 1731 he spent time in America, awaiting the decision on a grant for the project of a college in Bermuda which was in the end rejected. He became Bishop of Cloyne in 1734. He died in his lodging in Oxford while overseeing his son's introduction to Christ Church.

Berkeley completed his major visionary work as a young man, in his search to find a common sense in the world. This is contained in: *Essay towards a New Theory of Vision* (1709), *A Treatise Concerning the Principles of Human Knowledge* (1710), and *Three Dialogues between Hylas and Philonous* (1713). A major stimulus for his thoughts were the works of Locke, about whom he (as a young man) noted wryly that *Essay Concerning Human Understanding* was not published until Locke was sixty years old.

Locke's position held fast to the seventeenth century concept of science that the world was made up of mechanically related solid objects. These objects, again mechanically, act upon the human senses and cause "ideas" of those objects to be created in the mind of the perceiver and these ideas resemble the actual object that had caused them. Secondary senses of colours, tastes and so on are not ideal recreations of objects but are "modes" in the mind of the observer created by the stimulus of the perceived object. Berkeley thought this foolish, wondering how an observer, knowing only what was presented to him by his mind, could possibly "know" anything outside that. Also, if Locke's objective material world is eternal then, Berkeley thought, it does not need a creator and so no God. In addition, it is hard to sustain the idea of the mind as somehow different from the objective world as a "soul". And if this cannot be sustained then, for Berkeley, religion collapses and morality goes with it.

Berkeley strongly rejected Locke's idea of the universe as a massive machine of which we only have a poor image. The answer for Berkeley was simple, unavoidable and common sense—to deny the existence of matter. The objects of our senses have never been directly known to us, so removing them is not removing anything we have ever known. And doing this eliminates the inherent scepticism that some of these objects might not be exactly as they are perceived. But still "something" must exist, or the ideas we have would not be had. And this, according to Berkeley, is brought about in us by the will of God who sees and knows all things at all times. And if in this way there are no objects of the senses, then there can be nothing physical at all—"esse est percipi", "to be is to be perceived".

Berkeley's later work is less clear where, amongst other things, he gave his attention over to the medicinal and social benefits of tar water—"the drink that cheers but does not inebriate".

Berkeley's opinions were not regarded highly at a time when science was in its early and popular ascendancy. In the twenty-first century, with the grip of science embracing all forms of thinking, its standing has not improved.

As the captain of "The Enlightenment Philosophers' Seven-a-side Football Team", Berkeley can select the team on the basis of their sound ideas and can use his pastoral experience as a bishop to inspire them. His doubts about the existence of physical reality might have led to disaster in the game, but his faith in God sustains the team and he is able to reward them with suitable refreshment.

David Hume (1711-76)

Probably the greatest of all eighteenth century philosophers and a leading sceptical thinker of the enlightenment period, Hume, with his thoughts on logic, morality and politics, put forward a new interpretation of human nature. Throughout his work he attempts to reveal the limits of reason and the place of human inclination and understanding.

Setting himself the task of living a self-improving and frugal life, he left Scotland and settled in France from 1734-39 where he completed the first version of his most famous work *A Treatise of Human Nature*. Returning to London, he met with no success on the publication of the *Treatise*, only slight success with *Essays: Moral and Political*, failed to gain an academic post and struggled with badly chosen tutorships and precarious finances. Despite these setbacks, he worked hard producing in 1748 a reworking of the *Treatise* as *Philosophical Essays Concerning Human Understanding* (which, when published in 1758, became *An Enquiry Concerning Human Understanding*) and in 1751 *An Enquiry Concerning the Principles of Morals*. In the same year his *Dialogues Concerning Natural Religion* appeared. After this his interests and published work were concerned more with politics and history. In his fifties he returned to Paris between 1763-66. He returned to his home town of Edinburgh in 1769 where he remained, until bravely facing his death from bowel cancer in 1776.

Hume tackled all areas of philosophical enquiry that have application to the way that we view the world.

In logic and metaphysics he divided what we know into "impressions" and "ideas": impressions are the sensations we have of the world, ideas are the images we have of these.

Our beliefs, he thought, do not derive from causal relations deduced from reason and experience based upon a uniformity of nature. "Demonstrative" reasoning based on deduction does not meet the challenge as deductive reasoning can conceive of non-uniformity. Neither does "probable" reasoning which depends on previous probabilities. Instead our beliefs are based on habit and so are a product of the imagination. Inductive reasoning is what we rely on as it seems to correspond with what occurs in nature. Causation is therefore the "regular succession" of necessarily connected occurrences.

Hume rejected the idea that we have a simple, identical form as an individual. Rather, we are a bundle of perceptions succeeding each other in rapid and continual flux. His scepticism, however, is set aside in favour of an attitude of common sense which accepts the undertakings of life as we find them. He separates our ability to philosophise as a different pursuit.

For Hume beauty brings about feelings of pleasure in anyone that sees a certain object. The owner of the object, however, can feel something in addition—a sense of pride. The same applies to love, though this will involve another person, not an object. Morality, like beauty is for Hume something we can experience or have feelings about more than we can make judgement about. Morals derive from passions of varying intensity, not reason. Agreeable features in someone will involve sympathy, and such qualities experienced by others will bring about sympathetic pleasure.

His definition of miracles still stands, that a true miracle's "…falsehood would be more miraculous, than the fact which it endeavours to establish". For Hume, God cannot exist as an a priori truth because he is not known. Nor can He exist a posteriori as evidence from design is insufficient or poor. Because on miracles he offers convincing disavowal of their reality, and because the Christian religion is based on miracles, no reasonable person, he thought, can believe in it.

Hume's influence has been profound. His scepticism and its separation from simply living our lives gives a solid grounding for a thinking person's approach to a fulfilling life.

Hume takes a crucial part in "The Enlightenment Philosophers' Seven-a-side Football Team" with his ability to make observations and draw conclusions. His doubts about whether from these he is justified in going on to predict future events nearly lands the team in trouble, but his pragmatism enables him to carry on.

Baruch Spinoza (1632-77)

Spinoza, a leader in criticism of Biblical scriptures, opened the way in the recent history of Western philosophy to using philosophy as a means of living a full and purposeful life.

A member of a successful Jewish family living in Amsterdam, his mother died when he was six and his father when he was twenty-two. He was excommunicated from the Jewish faith for his heretical views. After several moves he settled in The Hague working as a lens grinder and, with some financial support from friends, he published anonymously what became his infamous *Tractatus Theologica-Politicus*. This politico-religious treatise put forward ways to attain complete freedom of thought for the individual while still abiding by the laws of the state. Here he designates the metaphysical claims of the Bible as mere embroidery of the main ethical message.

His hugely influential *Ethics* was published posthumously. It is set out in a Euclidean deductive framework with theorems proving the initial axioms and definitions. Here he deals with God, mind, emotions, strength of the emotions and human freedom. Following a complex argument, he defines God as being physical and nature itself. On balance he says that every physical thing has some form of sentience—a *conatus*—to actualise its self. In the human, an increase or decrease in the *conatus* is seen in the move across the range from pleasure to pain. Using this basis he analyses human psychology in a dispassionate manner.

Spinoza was a rigid determinist—the laws of nature, as God, determining everything throughout all history. But still the human can have freedom; active freedom (adequate ideas) stemming from its *conatus*, passive freedom (inadequate ideas) drawing on external things. Adequate ideas are closer to genuine knowledge. Knowledge moves through three phases: the lowest form utilising hearsay and vague experience, the next stage using reasoning, the final stage using intuitive, rationally based insight. The lowest form enslaves us, but we can move up the scale to the highest form of knowledge and so freedom when we realise "intellectual love of God".

Spinoza accepted that some individuals will never be able to reach the stage of experiencing the philosophical love of God, and for those religion may prove a morally worthy substitute. In this way Spinoza provides a meaningful and applicable philosophy for life. In his time he was seen as calling for abandonment of traditional Christian and Jewish views, though he was later recognised as an atheistic forerunner of absolute idealism. Himself influenced by Descartes, he has affected the thinking of, amongst others, Hegel, Nietzsche, Russell, Einstein and Freud and ranks amongst the foremost influences in modern thought on the nature and place of the individual.

In our verses here the philosophers Descartes, Berkeley, Hume, Spinoza, Leibniz, Kant and Locke take to the field as an unlikely and anachronous football team and some of their ideas begin to interfere with their ability to play effectively.

The Enlightenment Philosophers' Seven-a-side Football Team

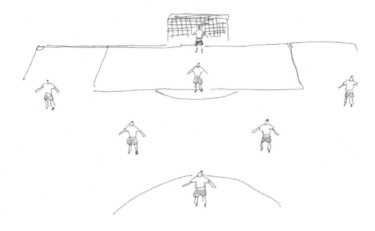

It were Berkeley's idea to develop a team,
To be the team captain had long been his dream;
He knew he'd have trouble assembling his squad,
But, being a bishop, he trusted to God.

For t'position of keeper he thought of Descartes;
It were him, after all, who had made a head-start
In solving the puzzle about what we know:
If we think, we exist, and that must be so.

For full-backs he thought first of Baruch Spinoza,
A bit of a rebel, a bit of a poser,
But solid in holding that all of us should
Make our own way through reason to find what is good.

Then Gottfried Leibniz would be strong in defence;
For him God was perfect; he argued from hence
That the world we are in is the best it can be,
And what God allows us is what we can see.

For wing forward Berkeley first thought of John Locke;
He'd be swift in attack and well able to block.
His obedience to t'captain would always be there
As long as t'captain's demands remained fair.

The other wing forward could be David Hume,
Tho' his irreligion had made Berkeley fume.
Hume could use his "impressions" to follow the play,
And then form "ideas" that might help win the day.

And right at the front, then, Immanuel Kant
(Though Berkeley's perception of him was quite scant);
He believed things that we think that we know
Depend on us knowing, conceiving them so.

The game had begun and Berkeley kicked off,
But he missed the ball, and giving a cough,
Said, 'It's not really there—we should have asked God
To attend to our game and all of the squad.'

So he said a quick prayer before sending the ball
In a high backward pass to Descartes in goal.
Descartes, in two minds, sent the ball to his right,
But Locke wasn't thinking, and lost it from sight.

Leibniz picked it up and prepared for a throw,

His knowledge innate about where it should go;
He aimed it to Kant, but he didn't share
Leibniz' space, time or ball and so it went spare.

The other side lost it, but then so did Hume,
For he tripped on the thought that he could not assume
That the ball always *would* reach the back of the net;
No principle says past behaviour is set.

John Locke tackled then, and resumed the attack
With his own style of play, and sent the ball back
To George Berkeley who dribbled it on to Spinoza,
Who signalled for Kant to come a bit closer.

Kant readied himself to receive a high pass;
Prepared for an ideal ball, but the mass
Of the ball on his head seemed to him more than real
A thing in itself, "noumena", he could feel.

This thought contradicted his long-held belief;
He stumbled, but though hesitation was brief,
The other side took up the chance that they saw
To reach the enlightenment goal and to score.

George Berkeley cried out, 'Come on lads, get a grip;
You know you can do more than stumble and trip;
Our ideas on knowledge may not all agree
But reason's our strength and we'll win yet, you'll
see!'

The other side reached the enlightenment end

But Spinoza tackled, the ball took a bend;
His opponent appeared to make use of his hands.
Descartes cried, 'There's no cause for doubt, t'foul
stands!'

The free kick was given which Spinoza took;
He sent it to Leibniz who darted a look
At John Locke before turning and heading to Hume
Who had run to the wing, where he'd plenty of room.

Hume kicked it to Kant who was nearing the goal;
The enlightenment team was now on a roll.
The referee, running up, looked at his watch;
And Kant knew this one chance he must not now botch.

He was onside, the ball at his feet, and he saw
That reason alone now would not help him score;
The team's universal approval was set—
His imperative kick reached the back of the net!

The team celebrated t'traditional way
With kisses and hugs, then Berkeley said, 'Hey!
We deserve some refreshment, I've got some right here.
It's my healthy tar water, the drink that brings cheer!'

Samuel Johnson (1709-84)

Dr Samuel Johnson's life and attitudes are recorded with great humour by James Boswell (1740-95). As far as his philosophising is concerned, he is best known for his refutation of Berkeley's idealism by kicking a stone and saying, "I refute it thus".

In the verses here, this stone-kicking is recalled but with a gastronomic bent.

Joseph Priestley (1733-1804)

A utilitarian, theological and political philosopher, Priestley preceded Bentham and J.S. Mill with ideas about bringing together the principle of utility with democratic freedom. He expounded what later became a Benthamite creed of calculating the greatest happiness for the greatest number of people. To bring about a reconciliation between the interests of the government and the interests of the people, and to prevent revolt, Priestley believed that the government must always appeal to the needs of the people: only by this means, he thought, can a government be properly restrained.

Born into a time of much natural discovery, Priestley was also a scientist and invented carbonated water and discovered oxygen. His commitment to the phlogiston theory (phlogiston being the supposed constituent that burns away on combustion) and the new chemical science of the time caused him to be isolated within this new scientific community. Because of his radical views he was in 1791 forced to flee to the United States.

In "A Philosophical Lunch" he is another philosopher at a time when he may have known about Berkeley and whom Bentham decided to invite to the memorial lunch. Unfortunately his scientific work keeps him away.

Jeremy Bentham (1748-1832)

Bentham considered thoughts and ideas in the fields of law, economics, politics and philosophy. He attracted a group of followers he called "Utilitarians". He prescribed that his body should be placed in a glass case after he died as what he called an "auto-icon". In this form he still attends some Benthamite meetings and the rest of the time sits in a corridor at University College, London.

Trained as a lawyer, Bentham quickly turned his enquiries into the nature and not the practice of the law. Although publishing some minor work at an early stage, the remainder of his work was edited and published by others, often being translated into French and re-translated into English. Much of his huge collection of unpublished work continues to be the subject of the Bentham Project.

Bentham's aim was to find a perfect system of law and for the grounding of this he constructed the idea of Utilitarianism—the "greatest happiness principle". Mankind, he believed, is guided by "two sovereign masters—pain and pleasure"—and it is only using the right law, governed by reason, that happiness can be achieved.

The rightness of actions is measured by their utility—the maximisation of pleasure and the minimisation of pain—and this is known by the consequences those actions produce.

Bentham was dedicated to the practice of utility. His ideas ranged from trains of carts running from London to Edinburgh, a Panama Canal, the freezing of peas and the privately run prison, the Panopticon. This was to have had a circular design where the guards could continually observe the prisoners—a "mill for grinding rogues honest". After a twenty year struggle and loss of his own money trying to get it built, the idea was finally turned down.

He believed that the individual could be led by appropriate government to work towards the greater good for all. Failure to do this must lead to punishment which, he believed, should only cause pain if that is greater than the crime caused when it was committed, or as a deterrent where people are deterred from doing things that would produce more pain, for example murder or theft.

His realisation that the chance of having enlightened government was unlikely led to him supporting the idea of a democracy on a one man, one vote, secret ballot principle. The more people that are involved in the democratic process, he thought, the more people would be working towards the greatest good for the greatest number. Although he supported the struggle for reform in both France and America, he did not support their revolutionary methods. He did not believe in a social contract that expected simple obedience to the law of the government, thinking instead that the individual should act on the utility principle of whether it is obedience or resistance that causes the greater harm.

In order to analyse the process of rights and duties, and finding nothing in place that worked, Bentham invented a system he called "paraphrasis". This is a method of not analysing concepts by looking at individual words, but by placing them in sentences, then using alternative sentences not containing the original word. From this analysis may emerge a real "entity" that can be clearly understood.

Bentham did not believe there was any such thing as "natural rights", thinking them imaginary. Real rights, he thought, could only be produced by actual systems of law. He argued that we should not be confused by believing in rights we think actually exist when in fact they are only rights we think ought to exist. His criticism of such a mistaken view is captured in his slogan "nonsense upon stilts".

Bentham's consequentialist theories, always look at the future possible good or harm, not at any good or harm caused in the present. On this basis he rejects common law based on history which he believed should be replaced by statute law made by democratically elected Parliaments and arrived at by reason. His thinking has had a massive influence on political and social thinking, and the ideas of utility and consequence guide much of modern thinking on moral behaviour in an ordered society.

In our verses here a young Bentham is imagined trying to arrange a lunch for philosophers and thinkers contemporaneous with him who might also have known of Berkeley. Unfortunately they all give their excuses, but Bentham is comforted by the thought that he has tried to follow his own policy of maximising happiness at least in the intention.

A Philosophical Lunch

In seventeen hundred and seventy-three,
The flow'ring of Britain's Philosophy,
George Berkeley'd been dead for nigh on twenty year
And his friends thought a jolly would give them some
cheer.

'Twas Bentham who first of all mooted the plan
And soon he had listed some guests, and began
To write letters to all in his spidery hand;

For some lived abroad in a faraway land.

Immanuel Kant was invited to come
And Bentham wrote, 'Pleasure? I think there'll be some;
The pain of the journey will soon be repaid
By meeting admirers of works that you made.'

But Kant was regretful, his RSVP
Said imperative reasons meant he was not free;
He had made it a rule, "categoric'lly so,
To home never leave, or to travelling go."

So Bentham tried others, Joe Priestley in Leeds,
Whose ideas he'd found out could chime well with his creeds;
Original thinker, a chemist as well
With plenty of after-lunch stories to tell.

But Priestley replied he was busy just now,
And went on to give his excuses and how
He had nearly succeeded dephlogisting air
And to halt the experiment would not be fair.

Next came Dr Johnson (and sidekick Boswell),
Whose diction'ry so many copies would sell.
He laughed as he struck a large rock with his toe
And quipped, 'Will a lunch still exist if I go?'

Now Bentham was worried; he'd hired them a room.
The last letter went to the Scot David Hume.

He'd known Berkeley's works and had followed his
line;
Surely this fact alone would compel him to dine.

But Hume was now frail and replied that the fact
Of his debt to George Berkeley was no cause to act;
'A statement of *is* cannot lead on to *ought,*
And the journey to England would kill me, it's thought.'

So Bentham was left to toast Berkeley alone
And to ponder upon some ideas of his own;
He'd done right to plan and to write to his friends,
Utility lies in the good of our ends.

Gottfried Wilhelm Leibniz (1646-1716)

Leibniz is recognised as the leading rationalist philosopher of the late seventeenth century believing, along with Plato and Descartes, that true a priori knowledge could be discovered by rational thought as opposed to experiment. Not a trained philosopher, he investigated all areas of human interest, publishing in his lifetime one book, *The Theodicy* together with a great range of articles and correspondence with leading and influential figures of the time. He "discovered" calculus at the same time as Newton, the modern evaluation of that being that Newton discovered it first but Leibniz published first. His other interests led him into alchemy, machinery design, the law and diplomacy.

Leibniz' metaphysics concerning his concept of "monads" finds best expression in his later more mature metaphysical work. Monads are the simple substances of which all things of matter are made and they are only known by perception. In addition, anything which involves motion in space is a phenomenon reliant upon the perception of a percipient, and that percipient's agreement with others about its nature.

Leibniz recognised that his theory of monadic perception was at odds with common sense. He defended this conflict using the thesis of "universal expression" wherein each monad can perceive all of the monads in various degrees, and of "pre-established harmony" in that God had created all things with the ability to perceive all other monads so, even though they don't causally react with one another, they have the ability to do so. He disagreed with Descartes' identification of matter with extension, instead holding that force cannot be identified with the extension of matter, but arises from its basic, substantial and immaterial form.

He also had concerns about the difficulties the human mind has in dealing with "free choice". On the basis of "infinite" analysis, he denied that "conceptually true" propositions are true because their "truth" relies upon the inclusion of unproved predicates. On the other hand he defended "necessarily true" propositions because there is always a "finite" analysis possible of their concepts.

Leibniz contributed to the theistic problem of evil using what he termed "theodicies". Defining God as omnipotent, omnipresent, omniscient and good, he upheld God's omnipotence and moral perfection. He based his a priori version of the cosmological argument on the principle that whatever is the case must be based on "sufficient reason" for it to be that way rather than another. As the world obviously is the way it is, then it must have a sufficient reason and this must be a necessary being who lies outside the world—God. So, God must have a sufficient reason for creating this world, and as God is good, then this world must be the "best possible" world. If it is possible that a perfect being like God could exist as a perfect being with every possible perfection, then in this way perfection is a simple property held by a perfect being.

Epistemologically he argued against Locke, upholding the argument that the mind is not a blank slate but is imbued from its origin with innate ideas and concepts. In addition, based on the idea of "concept containment", Leibniz offered alternatives to Aristotelian logic.

In "The Enlightenment Philosophers' Seven-a-side Football Team", Leibniz takes a strong defensive position supporting the idea that a perfect God has ensured that the world we inhabit is the best it can be.

In "G.W. Leibniz Services Ltd "No Job Too Big"" Leibniz advertises his many interests and abilities in the hope of obtaining employment suited to them.

G.W. Leibniz Services Ltd "No Job Too Big"

Established 1668,
I work in many trades;
My terms are fair, my hourly rate
Is set at several grades.

My basic or monadic fee
Is for the spark of thought,
And as I'm very bright, you see,
It will be dearly bought.

And then you pay for what I do—
The list is broad and long;
I think that there are very few
In which I am not strong:

There's alchemy; I found a way
To make potassium;
What's in your chamber pot today
Will serve to make you some.

And then, if you require a list
Of books on many shelves,
I catalogue—none will be missed—
You can't do that yourselves.

Perhaps you hate to multiply,
Divide, subtract or add?
My new machine will get you by
Without you going mad.

Or if you want to calculate
The space beneath a curve,
My calculus you're bound to rate

For it will surely serve.

I know the law and can advise

On action or dispute;
My clients know that I am wise
And win for them their loot.

You may own mines and feel the need
To get the water out;
My windmill pump does that with speed,
Of that there is no doubt.

I give advice to heads of state
Who should succeed them when
Their reign ends, as will be their fate,
And what will happen then.

For testimonial apply
To many patrons past;
And I am sure that they'll reply,
'His stock in trade is vast.'

For an appointment call me now,
I'll start the job today;
I must keep busy—on the go;
That's how I get my pay.

Immanuel Kant (1724-1804)

Kant is probably the most important post-Cartesian philosopher of modern times. He lived his whole life in Königsberg in East Prussia where he was educated in the quasi-Scholastic tradition focusing on the works of Wolff and Leibniz. His reading of David Hume turned his thought to penetrating the meaning and place of metaphysics. Opposing the rationalist view that everything can be understood using reason and the empiricist view that all knowledge is based on experience, Kant developed a wholly new concept that the external world could rely for its meaning on the observer. His most important contribution belongs to what is commonly referred to as his third period with the bringing to publication of his masterpiece *The Critique of Pure Reason*. Here he highlights the boundaries of metaphysics by demonstrating the contradiction of a priori and synthetic—metaphysics' claim that necessary truths cannot be based on empirical evidence (a priori), while at the same time relying on an analysis of their concepts (synthesis). "God exists", for example, is an analytic a priori statement, whereas "God is good" is synthetic.

He also considered reason flawed when it reached beyond experience with attempts to solve puzzles such as cosmology, time and space, infinity and causation. Kant saw that it was possible to construct valid arguments that could both uphold and deny metaphysical questions. Unless synthetic a priori knowledge is shown to be possible and there is successful resolution of these contradictions—"antimonies"—he deemed metaphysics impossible. To resolve this, Kant turned our usual way of thinking on its head: instead of our knowledge conforming to the world of objects we should, he said, see objects as conforming to our ways of knowing. In this way, for Kant, the world is not a "knowing" of true objects but only a "sensation" of them, as they appear to us. We therefore live in a world of "phenomena", being able to think of the "noumenal" world of objects but never being able to know it. This "transcendental idealism" allows for the possibility of the synthetic a priori knowledge of objects since such objects must naturally conform to however they appear as objects to us. By this means Kant invalidates traditional metaphysics ,which deals with matters that cannot be answered by appeal to experience.

From this, proposing that humans could be part of the noumenal world and so be free, he develops his moral theory based on the idea of the "categorical imperative" —a moral rule that, if adopted universally, can be accepted as right by all. However, Kant also proposes moral antimony where personal freedoms are subjugated to the will of the categorical imperative. Indeed, his concentration on the fundamental matters of human freedom and reasoning about action lead to his view being much criticised for its concentration on rules and duties while not accounting for happiness, virtuousness and relationships between individuals. Testing out the categorical imperative brings about many contradictions and still it remains unclear whether these have been fully resolved.

Kant's appearance as striker in "The Enlightenment Philosophers' Seven-a-side Football Team" sees him exchanging a considered approach to football for a more inspired and spontaneous desire to put the noumenal ball in the back of the net. And, as an unforeseen bonus he reveals his ability to take the ball

on his head—"He's got a good head on him, that boy!",
his mother always quite rightly observed.

In "Immanuel (Mannie) Kant: Agony Aunt" we find
Kant as "Aunt Mannie" answering letters from
troubled correspondents in the popular magazine "The
Königsberg Imperative".

Immanuel (Mannie) Kant: Agony Aunt

Dear Mannie, I am in a mess,
It's really got me down;
I am a man I must confess,
But like to wear a gown.

I put on lipstick and some heels
And go to town at night;
You've no idea how good it feels,
But am I doing right?

Crossdresser, thanks for writing in,
I think I understand;

You're worried what you do is sin,
But let me lend a hand:

It may seem natural to you
To wear a woman's dress,
But whether it is *right* to do
Requires more than a guess.

Imagine if all men decide
To crossdress every night;
And no-one thinks he needs to hide,
But feels that it is right.

Would this make what you do okay
Or would it spoil the fun?
Perhaps you're happy being gay
And not like everyone.

You see, when we are going to act
We need to reason thus:
Do we desire that all, in fact,
Must do the same as us?

To know you're right in what you do,
This maxim you must say;
"I wish that all men take the view
Cross-dressing is the way."

Thomas Hobbes (1588-1679)

Thomas Hobbes shared the company of Francis Bacon, Galileo and Descartes, claimed fearfulness as a personal asset, translated ancient Greek texts and published work in support of both sides of the English Civil War. He was a controversial figure throughout his long life.

Hobbes was a materialist, contributing to psychology where he gave an explanation for pleasure and pain as expressions of innate attributes of the appetite under the heading of "endeavour". He does not link these with his materialist view, saying that the answer to the appetites or aversions can be found by introspection. Similarly, he finds no incompatibility between determinism, freedom and God's power—as long as we act according to our "will" then we act freely. Hobbes believes that people can act well and for the good but thinks this is not common. But reason and the passions can work together when directed towards the avoidance of pain or suffering, though it is only reason that can plot a course towards long term goals whereas passion is only fitted for short term satisfaction. But importantly, irrational action can satisfy the need to avoid life-threatening accident or pain. This fitting together of the apparently incompatible elements passion and reason has great appeal to a common sense understanding of human conduct. Hobbes considers the preservation of the person the essential virtue and this, utilising the "good manners" of appropriate moral behaviour, can lead to the individual living at peace and so to everyone living at peace.

The right to nature as "brutish and short" has to be given up to the use of reason. When applied to long-term goals, such reason can help shape an appropriate society for everyone. Even so, the individual is still entitled to passion-led responses, and, above all, the right to self-defence is paramount. With such a system in place, the individual can be obliged to the law of the state while still having rights of his own. Hobbes' version of the social contract entered into by the individual with the sovereign is seen as a gift given to ensure preservation of the individual in a peaceful; society. Both the sovereign and the individual are obliged to the commitment to ensuring the safety of the people.

His formulation and description of the 'social contract' between the individual and the state remain a pattern against which political and socio-ethical thinking can be measured.

The verses "Hobbes and Locke Advise on Setting up an Orphanage School" concern the hatching of a plan by Hobbes and the much younger Locke to start an orphanage school. Obviously how and at what stage in life the children should be educated is a cause of some entrenched disagreement.

John Locke (1632-1704)

Locke was at the forefront of early post-Cartesian enlightenment philosophy, and was a critic of much Cartesian thinking. He wrote on all the main subjects of philosophy as well as education, economics, medicine and politics (his involvement with which led to a six year exile in Holland (1683-89).

Locke's contribution covers all areas of natural philosophy: the relation of terms to substances in the world, how we come to define things according to the ways our ideas of them are formed, the idea of knowledge in itself and how this contrasts with beliefs, opinions and what we might consider a priori truths.

Believing in the goodness of human nature (as opposed to Hobbes who interestingly thought it bad), Locke developed the idea of living in a "state of nature". He emphasised the consensual nature of the social membership of the individual who could choose to belong to small independent groups with a well-developed system of consent to agreed laws.

Locke's belief in God guided his epistemology. He denied innate knowledge, believing it instead to be always derived from experience and the use of reason. For Locke, we are born with a clean slate and, as we develop, rationalism is the only way of extricating us from simple belief.

He closely analysed our "ideas" of the objective world, importantly distinguishing the simple and indefinable from the complex constructed out of the simple.

He recognised that even though "natural philosophy" cannot be made a science, this is no reason for pessimism. He took a common sense view that most of what we know in the way that we know it is sufficient for our normal purposes of living. He believed, however, that neither geometry nor ethics can be accepted as real: geometry deals with essences, not substances; ethics can be substantiated by the Bible, though this of course, requires faith and faith is outside rational thinking which always needs to be applied if any true knowledge is to be found.

Locke has helped shape not only epistemology, but also psychology. His view on the meaning of "pure substance" is still part of live philosophical discussion, as are his thoughts on personal identity and its continuity. His method of analysis was followed by the consequently influential philosophies of both Priestley and J.S. Mill. His ideas on checks and balances in government were foundational for the US constitution, and his encouragement for free enterprise and his analysis of the problems associated with state government are still part of political thinking.

In "The Enlightenment Philosophers' Seven-a-side Football Team", Locke appears as first choice for wing forward. Quite rightly Berkeley, as team captain, perceives Locke's sharpness of mind and his speed and commitment to the team. Indeed, this recognition causes Locke's qualities to "be".

In "Hobbes and Locke Advise on Setting up an Orphanage School", Locke works with Hobbes to plan a school. However, his ideas of what would make a good one differ from those of Hobbes'.

Hobbes and Locke Advise on Setting up an Orphanage School

John Locke knew some people, some really rich nobs
With titles and what not—and so did Tom Hobbes.
These folk got together, resources to pool,
Intent on creating an orphanage school.

Lord Cavendish was an old patron of Hobbes;
He'd used him for family tutoring jobs.
Locke's friend was Lord Ashley who gratefully said
That without Locke's assistance as doc, he'd be dead.

Ashley and Cavendish needed advice
On founding the school, and they named a good price.
Though Hobbes nearly eighty, and Locke thirty five,
They'd chosen those two men to make the scheme
thrive.

So John Locke and Tom Hobbes began on their task;
And first of all found that they needed to ask
How places like this one were set up and ruled
For those little children to come and be schooled.

John said, 'A child's mind is just like a blank slate
Which we need to write on before it's too late;
For early impressions are the ones that endure
So they have to be rooted in grounds that are sure.'

'A child does need training,' came Tom Hobbes' reply,
'For he's born concerned only with "Me, Myself, I";
If left to himself he'll not grow as he ought,
And his life will be poor, nasty, brutish and short.'

But Locke, while respectful, did not share this view:

'We each can be selfish, but I think it's true
That tol'rance and reason are ours from the start
And we'll then work with others to play our own part.

If children are placed into groups that are small,
They'll soon find a way to deal fairly with all;
Their teachers can lead them and help them to learn
Through co-operation and taking their turn.'

Hobbes could not agree with this vision of Locke:
'Just think how an orphan would deal with the shock
Of the loss of his parents who'd kept him from fear,
Then left him to fight any threat that came near.

In this state of nature he'd resist being ruled
By a liberal method of getting him schooled;

Instead he'd need laws, though against them he'd chafe,
And a power like a parent's would make him feel safe.'

Said Locke, 'If we could but discover the man,
This paragon person, this Leviathan
To order the children so they'd feel secure,
We'd have solved at least half of the problem for sure.'

'The rest of the problem that troubles us here,'
Said Hobbes, 'now presents as abundantly clear;
To resolve what remains both our minds we must turn:
How and what do we think that the children should
learn?'

'My idea', replied Locke, is to start them at three
(When they're young and receptive as you can well
see),
And to start them on learning a trade that will soon
Bring in money from garden or spindle or loom.

They can start with the proceeds to buy their own
bread,
(As well save t'school costs of getting them fed);
The natural motive their living to earn
Will give them the reason and focus to learn.'

So Tom Hobbes and John Locke submitted their plan
For their patrons to stump up and find the right man
To set up a school the vocational way;
And they waited to see what these worthies would say.

Lord Cavendish said, 'Oh, I'd wanted to see
A plan that's prestigious, reflecting on me;
To have children working and learning a trade
Would not show the world all the wealth that I've
made.'

Lord Ashley regretted he'd have to withdraw
His support for the project, even though for the poor.
'I am standing for office and think that, as such,
A link with this school will not help me much.'

And he said, 'Such a scheme is ahead of its time;
Perhaps in due course there will be the right clime
For vocational schooling; until that day comes,
It's enough to do reading and writing and sums.'

So the school never happened and old Hobbes and
Locke,
Their joint plan rejected, were left to take stock:
Sound knowledge and argument can recommend,
But money and power will decide in the end.

Jean-Jaques Rousseau (1712-78)

Rousseau is credited as the designer of the "social contract" which promotes sovereignty of the state via the intention of the general will of the citizens. This encourages both "liberty" and "equality", and in the process, "fraternity". "Man is born free; and everywhere he is in chains" has become the rallying cry for many revolutionary movements ever since. Rousseau believed man is essentially good and it is the actions of the society to which he belongs that bring about corruption. His work extends beyond political thought to education, music and fiction, and the ideas contained in *Social Contract* and *Émile* are his lasting legacies. He created controversy during his lifetime and the question of whether he is a liberator of the individual or a promoter of totalitarianism is still controversial.

"Free Supply" focuses on the educational ideas of Rousseau, which seem to be able to be put into effect over his dead body..

Free Supply

Jean-Jacques Rousseau, a long time dead,
Was not allowed to lie;
When staff were short, an agent head
Unearthed him for supply.

The times were hard and government
Had called on the retired,
And neither death not interment
Barred them from being hired.

Jem Bentham, stuffed and well-preserved,

Had filled a council post;
And UCL had been well served—
He'd longer worked than most.

Jean-Jacques was highly qualified
For Music, French and Art;
A little Civics on the side
And he could play his part.

They propped him up in Year 10 French
And left him for the hour;
Their noses wrinkled at the stench:
His grave-clothes were quite sour.

His teaching plan was from *Émile*:
He simply sat and stared;
The pupils then began to feel
An impulse that they shared:

They could explore and find alone
The way they could best learn;
Experience their skills would hone
And for them wisdom earn.

The language lab was well resourced,
Each pupil had his place;
And no one needed to be forced
But learned at his own pace.

Results for French that year were good
And OFSTED gave high praise,
But had concerns, as so it should,
About the teacher's ways:

'His manner's lifeless, still and cold,
He never breathes a sound,
He is, if we can make so bold,

Pungent to be around.

We wonder also if it's true
He's had no DBS
And, now we're not in Europe too,
His status is a guess.

The matter's grave, and for the school,
However well he teaches,
You have to stay within the rule,
Avoid these kinds of breaches.'

The agency did not agree:
'The law binds those who give
Their birthright up of being free
For sustenance to live.

But Rousseau, as you must have found,
Needs neither warmth nor bread;
No social contract has him bound,
No laws constrain the dead.'

The agency put in no claims,
They let old Rousseau be;
The wage-slave's life is bound by chains—
Only the dead are free.

John Stuart Mill (1806-73)

Mill was the foremost British philosopher of the nineteenth century, combining the traditions of liberalism and empiricism and raising them to new heights. Contributing great works such as *On Liberty* and *Utilitarianism*, serving briefly as a Member of Parliament and, amongst other causes, strongly supporting women's rights, Mill sought through his philosophy to blend the Enlightenment and Romanticism.

As a phenomenalist he expressed, as "eliminative induction", doubt of the existence of real objects and acknowledged that all we know are mental experiences. Metaphysically he thought that as mind is part of nature, then there can be no a priori knowledge of the natural world. As such, science must be built entirely on experience. He believed that external objects are merely "permanent possibilities of sensation", that is, always remaining available to sensation, and that mind is a series of sensations which are somehow known by the self (though he does not deal with the difficulties arising from this being in a temporal order).

Mill's work covers the full range of human experience, describing human nature as the foundation upon which the complete individual could be formed. As an empiricist he believed that true knowledge could be discovered by analysis of the world as opposed to simply thinking about it. He worked out an ethical theory based on the consequences of action, not upon obligation to duties. This means calculating the potential effects of all the various courses available ,then, as a result of adding up all the possible happiness and unhappiness for everyone involved, taking the course that should bring about the greatest overall happiness.

He maintained that everyone should be free to conduct their own "experiments of living" as long as they do not harm anyone else. He argued for sexual equality of opportunity, believing that as long as there is equality of opportunity, although some differences would remain, those differences would not be prejudicial to either sex.

These ideas combine together into what we now call "Utilitarianism", an idea originated by Jeremy Bentham and taken up and developed by Mill. For both of them the ultimate aim of moral action is hedonistic (an increase in happiness). However, even though they had different views about what happiness is—Bentham thought it a blissful state, whereas Mill believed it to be found on an ascending scale of lower to higher pleasures, the more refined pleasures (for example, music or art) being higher on the scale—they both believed that "amounts" or "degrees" of happiness could be calculated. Following this line he believed that education and experience can enhance our understanding of happiness. For the individual, Mill's utilitarianism says we should be able to do anything we choose, extending Bentham's utilitarianism and advocating the personal freedom of the individual in his own home against any interference by the state or others (even if interference may be considered for his own mental or physical good) unless it is to prevent harm to others.

Mill's utilitarianism promotes the individual's right to freedom of thought, speech, individuality and rejection of religious authority. Indeed, Mill takes a strong "anti-state" view which combines the ethical and the descriptive-explanatory views in a form which, like

Rousseau, attempts to blend the needs of both the individual and (to a lesser extent) the state. Mill's main reason for allowing the state to coerce its population is in order to protect one individual from harming another. He makes interesting exclusions to state coercion, for example the very young, the very old or societies that have themselves become "old". Mill does not sanction controlling the person for "his own good". He advocates selecting political leaders with exceptional skills and morality. His liberal individualism does not support the role of the majority; instead it promotes a system that is able to represent the wishes of minorities. Mill believed that extra votes should be given to those with superior intelligence.

In summary, Mill's ethical utilitarianism finds a place for the individual in which he can express himself fully, not interfere with others, and achieve the highest level of happiness while at the same time playing a part in an ordered, non-coercive and morally led state.

In "Putting Westminster Through the Mill", Mill laments the fact that some of the changes he thought essential to British politics have still not been implemented by the twenty-first century.

Putting Westminster Through the Mill

In Westminster, at midnight, all was still
But for the ghostly form of J.S.Mill;
He'd haunted both the houses since the day
He'd sat for Westminster and had his say.

And as he went he shook his head and groaned,
'Fifty and a hundred years,' he moaned,
'I'd really looked by now for much more change:
The books I've left set out a goodly range:

There's suffrage, and I cannot help but note
That more folk, aye and women, have the vote;
But still it is as 'twas: "first past the post",
And simple counting who has got the most.

This makes so many voters turn away,
Believing they can never have a say;
The government will come to be resented
By those who've not been represented.

And what of those who are in Parliament?
Are they enlightened and of serious bent?
Do they try hard to increase happiness
For all, or feather only their own nest?

Are people free to say what's in their mind?
Progress depends on hearing every kind
Of view, and truth can only be revealed
When contrary opinions take the field.

I see that many members of the state
Are still condemned to miserable fate,
While those in power enjoy unequal shares

And pass entitlement down to their heirs.

I'd think that now the dispossessed would rise

And take possession of the state, the prize,
But they are enslaved by trinkets from abroad—
Bent on amassing what they can't afford.'

So spoke the wraith, and turning sadly, left
The place he'd haunted, feeling now bereft;
Westminster had failed his searching test,
Weighed down by years of vested interest.

Karl Heinrich Marx (1818-83)

Marx was born into an upper middle class Christian family in Trier, Germany. He studied successfully, first at Bonn then in Berlin. Here he gained his doctorate, befriended Friedrich Engels and came under the influence of the new Hegelians, active in Germany at that time.

Marx and Engels, while associating with the newly formed Communist League, wrote the *Communist Manifesto*. Marx fell foul of the authorities, his political opinions leading to his statelessness and exile. In 1848 he was ordered out of Germany. He fled to Paris where he was introduced to the working-class movement and, by Engels, to the study of political economy, but was expelled from there in 1849. In the same year he moved to London where, after some years of abject poverty during which his own health permanently suffered and three of his six children died, he spent the rest of his life.

Employed only as European correspondent for the *New York Times* for a meagre fee, he spent most of his time working and studying in the British Museum. He published Volume 1 of *Capital* in 1867, Engels editing Volumes 2 and 3 and publishing them in 1884 and 1893 respectively.

Influenced by the Hegelian movement, Marx drew on his doctoral work on the materialistic philosophies of Democritus and Epicurus. As a parallel of the working class struggle, Marx sought to bring together the concepts of German idealism and the materialism of the French Enlightenment's struggle to conquer the individual's alienation in a naturally alienating social climate. For Marx there is no point in religion as it provides only a sense of hope which, if absent, renders it meaningless. Instead, he believed that the fulfilling life could only be obtained through the free and active expression of the individual self. However, for members of the working class, this sort of fulfilment is not available as individuals are reduced to repetitive and meaningless tasks; the self-fulfilment belonging solely to the capitalist employer of their labour. In this way it is the marketplace, falsely revealing itself as an opportunity for individual freedom, which in fact enslaves the worker.

Marx believed in a continuously changing future communistic society where all class differences and private ownership are abolished, and the individuals' self-fulfilment will arise as the social causes of alienation are eliminated. The aim must be a change which alters the system so that true self-fulfilment is possible. For Marx the way to do this is not to work out a plan and then try and apply it, but to take part in an active class movement that develops and actualises its own goals as the revolutionary process proceeds.

Marx has had immense influence on social and political change in the world, and his thoughts on how the means of production can be best used for the benefit of the proletariat remain live issues. Marx is one of the most influential figures in modern social science and his work forms the basis for thinking on labour and capital which has influenced activists and politics ever since.

"Shopping with Marx and Spencer" imagines Marx needing a new coat. At the shop he is impressed by the cheapness of the material, but shocked to realise that its price could only have been achieved by the mass production techniques which alienate the workers. An

added irony arises from the fact that Marx, relying on the son of a capitalist (Engels) for supplements to his meagre income, finds himself making use of a system he believes to be historically doomed.

Herbert Spencer (1820-1903)

Known as the "father of Sociology", Spencer was a singular thinker who trod his own path. Spurning the works of others, claiming that reading disagreeable books gave him headaches, he set about expounding his philosophy in what became a prodigious written output.

Spencer proposed an extreme social Darwinism within which morality arises from evolution. On this principle nature always tends towards equilibrium and can be seen reflected in both evolution of types as well as social and political balancing. He was never popular in his day and as a staunch opponent of female suffrage, with an ever-growing conservatism and as a scathing critic of the Boer war, he was held in particularly low esteem in later years.

Like others with great talent, Spencer also found time to turn his mind to other things. A result was that he invented the "binding-pin"—the precursor of the modern day paper clip.

In "Shopping with Marx and Spencer", he is imagined finding fault with the price of a new tailor-made coat on the basis that mass production, which he believed was the inevitable next stage of industrial evolution, would have made it much cheaper.

Shopping with Marx and Spencer

'There's a hole in my jacket!' Karl Marx said one day;
'Get a new one,' said Jenny, his wife, 'but who'll pay?'
'I'll ask Friedrich Engels,' said Marx, 'he's the son
Of an owner of capital—you know the one.'

At the tailors they showed Marx a wonderful tweed;
Said Karl, 'This cloth is well woven indeed!
Please tell me the weaver who made it so nice
And was able to sell it at such a low price.'

'Oh, that's no lone weaver,' the tailor replied,
'This was made in a factory by t'riverside;
A man making tweed by himself would take ages
And expect a return for his time in his wages.

In t'factory taking on skilled men is out,
Their skills are redundant, and there is no doubt
That women are cheaper so they tend the looms
That work by steam power in multiple rooms.

And by mass production the cost is cut down

So the cloth I use making a jacket or gown
Is far cheaper to buy and then I can sell
What I make at a price suiting customers well.'

'This is crazy,' said Marx, 'If I buy one today
It may go in part to give workers their pay,
But t'factory owner will take off his share
Just for having the money to set it up there.

My friend Engel's father is just such a one
And taking his money, I can see what I've done:
I am feeding a system that's doomed to decay,
But that's in the future; I need some today.'

At much the same time another great man
Had also come up with a utopian plan.
His theories, however, were far from the same;
He was called Herbert Spencer and from Derby he
came.

This Spencer one day began feeling a chill
And, fearing (as often) that he might get ill,
He went off to town set on finding a coat
In St Michael Street, to a tailor of note.

He liked the thick wool the assistant had shown;
A bargain, he thought, but then having it sewn
Would add so much on that he was appalled
And insisted the top master tailor be called.

'Now look here, my man,' Herbert Spencer then said,
'Your prices are high and you're not go-ahead;
Production of garments bespoke in this way
Will be soon superseded by methods that pay.'

The tailor, polite, bowed but held his head high,
'It may be the future, but while people buy

The suits that my hours and mastery made
I can charge what it takes to remain in the trade.'

H. Spencer looked glum then before he replied,
'But man must evolve and take change in his stride;
And those that fail this, well, they'll go to the wall ;
For society's progress some weak men must fall.'

'A cruel fate for them,' the top tailor then said,
'And a change I hope only comes after I'm dead!
Meanwhile do you want a coat made from this wool?
It'll keep you from chills now the weather is cool.'

'I suppose that needs must', said H. Spencer, and
sighed,
'I'm a victim to chills and to much more beside;
I'll pay your high price now and hope that some day
Mankind will adapt my utopian way.'

Like Spencer and Marx we would all like a change
That would bring us advantage, but cannot arrange
For its timely arrival. We put up with our lot
And accept that the present is all we have got.

Friedrich Wilhelm Nietzsche (1844-1900)

Nietzsche trained as a classical philologist and, from holding a professorship at the age of only twenty-four at Basle University, has emerged from a short productive life as one of the foremost influences in modern philosophy.

Influenced by Schopenhauer's belief in a godless and irrational world in which the living were condemned to ceaseless struggles and suffering, Nietzsche set out to find some worth from this bleak nihilistic depiction and so overcome nihilism. His essays and works led to his experimental *Thus Spoke Zarathustra*, his autobiographical *Ecce Homo* and, collected together after his death, *The Will to Power*. Deeply concerned with the quality of life and culture in which he found himself, he sought to construct a future that would follow from what he believed to be in store: the "death of God" and the "advent of nihilism".

After a mental breakdown in 1889, he suffered from ever deteriorating health.

Nietzsche is commonly mistaken as a negative thinker. His largely aphoristic work continues forcibly to seek a positive way forward and out of the unavoidable collapse of traditional values, of metaphysics and scientific knowledge. His work testifies to a broad-based thinking method involving social, psychological and cultural interpretation. For him, morality and religion were weakening influences on human nature. Instead he saw the world as made up of continual change brought about by the "will to power" with no structure or final outcome. He believed man to be soul-less and part of nature where some would rise to the top as "overmen", while others, less exceptional, would remain part of the "herd". It would be from the efforts of this higher element of mankind that redemption from nihilism would be found. He argued for morality to be established by the "higher" types and emphasised the crucial role of art in the working out of such ideas.

Drawing on a wide variety of perspectives offers strength to his thinking which points a way to a godless world in which human nature can be appreciated while at the same time being used to further its own meaningful future. His philosophy, however, is not rigorous in the normal sense; instead, "making of cases" by offering up ideas and suggestions rather than reason-founded argument. He conceded that any conclusions he reached were not proofs but rather "his truths".

Nietzsche is not a nihilist. Questioning only values that he believed mask other more important values, his influence in modern philosophy is profound.

Our verses here concentrate more on his healthier early life, his immense moustache and his unsuccessful wooing.

Friedrich Nietzsche Replies to a Lonely Hearts Advertisement

My name is Friedrich Nietzsche,
But you can call me Fred;
I have a facial feature—
It's sure to knock you dead.

Now, facial hair's in fashion
And most men sport some fluff,
But mine you'll view with passion
If you like a bit of rough.

My occupations vary;
I teach, write and compose
And take care of the hairy
Outgrowth beneath my nose.

I'm looking for
another—
A strong, free-
thinking wench,
Who's fit to be the
mother
Of a future
Übermensch.

My age is four and
twenty—
Don't let that put you
off—
Of prospects I've got
plenty;
They've just made me a Prof!

I have no truck with morals—
They're for the common herd;
This has led to quarrels,
But I think that they're absurd.

I have a younger sister
Who tries to make me cower;
I find I must resist 'er
When she's a Will to Power.

My mother is a widow;
My father is long dead:
I'm the only man and so
I am the family head.

Looked at from any angle
I'm really quite a catch;
Don't let's delay or wrangle,
But see if it's a match.

Meet me at the corner;
Don't think you're being rash:
You'll know me as the owner
Of the world's biggest moustache.

A Feature of Nietzsche

A philosopher called Friedrich Nietzsche
Was known for one physical feature:
His monster moustache
For his girl cut a dash,
But she cried when his lips couldn't reach'er.

John McTaggart Ellis McTaggart
(1866-1925)

The world has given life to many great minds. McTaggart, as the last of the British idealists, ranks amongst the greatest. As a metaphysician there are few throughout the whole course of history who could be called his equal. He was a man of deep mystical insight and commitment, and the possessor of a powerful analytical mind; a combination which places him amongst those who have altered our way of thinking and to whom we are indebted.

He worked for many years on an exposition of Hegel and throughout his life he pursued an ontological course —philosophical investigation into existence or being— that led him to a bold metaphysical scheme. He believed strongly in our immortal existence as members of an all-loving universe.

McTaggart defined by the *A*, *B* and *C*-Series the psychological foundation for a view of time which opened previously locked doors. His paper "The Unreality of Time" that appeared in *Mind* in 1908 was considered of such importance that he was invited to The University of California, Berkeley, to deliver it. Since then no discussion on time can proceed without reference to his propositions. Undoubtedly Einstein and Heisenberg were aware of his work, and virtually every modern discussion on the subject makes reference to his terms.

As is sometimes the case in philosophy, McTaggart's thesis continues to be misunderstood or misinterpreted, commentators dwelling on his denial of time at the cost of not seeing what he replaces it with. Arguments against the so-called "B" theorists, that "B" theory cannot give an account of change, and against the "A" theorists that McTaggart's paradoxical conclusion (that time is unreal) is inescapable, dominate. But for McTaggart, his classification of the elements of time and his denial of its reality was only laying the ground for his main metaphysical scheme. This proposes the *C*-Series, as a psychologically appealing timeless world free from the confusing psychological models of temporality so often at odds with our experience. Here, ideal selves exist in a non-temporal series as part of a loving whole which will come to fruition at an end stage when the last perception is in place.

Surely there can be no greater tribute to a philosopher than that he actually believed in and lived by what he said. In this, McTaggart did his duty to the end. As a child he found no God. When he died, still godless, he welcomed the change that would lead him on to more of the loving immortality which he felt he knew was his future.

McTaggart's full contribution is yet to be acknowledged, though his impeccably constructed argument for an eternal yet timeless world of love lies ready for the future to receive.

Our verses here imagine McTaggart in what was known at the time as "The Mad Tea-Party of Trinity", comprising McTaggart (as the dormouse), Bertrand Russell and G.E. Moore. Lewis Carroll's Alice in Wonderland had been published in 1865, and was obviously well-known by the Cambridge academics who had presumably overheard the trio discussing such knotty problems as time.

Time for tea!

At Trinity, with table laid,
And sandwiches all freshly made,
There looked to be a princely tea,
But only room enough for three.

A hatter and a hare were there,
And, sleeping in another chair,
There was a dormouse snoring still;
Of sandwiches he'd had his fill.

The dormouse stirred and raised his head,
'You know, time is unreal,' he said.
The others laughed until they wept;
'So no time passed then, while you slept?'

'What passed and how?' the dormouse asked,
'I know with sleep my eyes were masked,
Perhaps you mean events have changed;

Before and *after* rearranged.'

The hare replied, 'Of course we mean
The situation that has been
Has brought us to this present stand
From which a future will expand.'

The dormouse yawned; 'That's series *A*.
Past, present, future, all should stay
Discrete and sep'rate one from t'other,
For if mixed up, we're in a bother.

If change occurs, then what was past
Becomes a present, slow or fast,
And will go on, early or late,
To yet another, future, state.'

The hare replied, 'But common sense
Tells us we live in time, and tense
Expresses what we know we feel:
Past, present, future— they are real!'

The dormouse sighed, 'They are not sound:
Our present has within its bound
The present future, as you see
When you plan out what's going to be.

And when your future comes in view
It also holds the past that you
Imagined for it, so in vain
You try to cleave the one from twain.'

'But does this mean,' the hatter asked,
'That humans are forever tasked
With living constantly in error?
This seems to me a holy terror!'
'That's Series *D*', t' dormouse replied,

'And in it we must all reside,
Experience outside this bound
Can be imagined, but not found.

So tell me this: can you explain
How—when we see events remain
Unchanged but *seem* to change from "were"
To "are", to "will"—can this occur?'

The hatter shook his greying locks,
'What we have here's a paradox:
To describe change in making sense
We employ tense to explain tense!

Then could a timeless world exist?
Said t'hatter as he clenched his fist,
'All that we know, the complete range,
Is mutable, subject to change!'

The dormouse smiled, nodded his head,
'A timeless world exists,' he said:
'Loving perceptions, series *C,*
Are outside place and time, you see.'

The other two were lost for speech,
These new ideas were out of reach;
But though they wanted so much more,
The dormouse recommenced to snore.

Bertrand Russell (1872-1970)

Hugely influential to the world of twentieth century philosophy, Russell throughout his long life developed not only a high academic reputation contributing to all fields of philosophical interest including its history, but found public notice in his autobiographical work, his high profile condemnation of war and long term work for the Campaign for Nuclear Disarmament.

A high ranking member of the aristocracy, he was a student of McTaggart's at Trinity College, Cambridge where he worked with G. E. Moore and Wittgenstein. His work contributed to the end of a strong tradition in British idealism.

Russell invented the phrase "philosophical logic" and, with Moore in the *Principia Mathematica,* tried to show how difficulties in philosophy could be dealt with by using a logical form of analysis. This he showed by describing how basic words stand for some corresponding entity. Ordinary language, he believed, led to so many errors and confusion that it became useless as a tool of analysis, enshrining the "superstitions of cannibals". This phrase however reveals his rather arrogant view that only those trained in thinking can expect to understand the world and their own thoughts about it. Not withstanding this, his legacy in this area remains.

He argues that mathematics has no distinct subject matter and can be "translated" into truths of pure logic. On this basis, anything that appears as mathematical, once translated into appropriate logical form, can be proved by logic alone. This idea has been attacked, notably by Gödel, and remains open to dispute.

In epistemology and metaphysics, Russell's "logical atomism" takes a Cartesian view that doubting things should be the method of enquiry, accepting only things that remain beyond doubt. This process takes place between the atomic construction of the real object of sense and the atomic construction of the one who is sensing. Scepticism about the true nature of the object is retained while at the same time having enough tangible information upon which to base scientific belief.

His later work allows for certain sorts of a priori knowledge though throughout, the abiding theme is that words correspond to and quantify some entity in the perceived world.

In "Bertrand Russell and Ludwig Wittgenstein Take a Punt in the Stream of Life", Russell is being teased by Wittgenstein on the basis of his assumption that words stand for some corresponding entity and can be understood by those suitably trained.

Ludwig Josef Johann Wittgenstein
1889-1951

In important respects probably the most influential philosopher of the twentieth century, Wittgenstein has shaped much of modern philosophy.

After studying engineering in both Berlin and Manchester, he went to Cambridge in 1912 to work with Bertrand Russell. He served in the First World War, and during this period wrote the only book published in his lifetime, the *Tractatus Logico Philosophicus*. In the early 1920's he came into contact with the "Vienna Circle" and this helped form his ideas on Logical Positivism. From 1929 he returned to teaching work at Cambridge, though never felt happy there. His work from then on reacted against his earlier work and, only finding expression in his contact with others, was not published until two years after his death from prostate cancer in 1953 as *Philosophical Investigations*.

Rejecting both traditional alternatives offered by philosophy and the common presuppositions of everyday thinking, Wittgenstein offered instead an analytical approach dealing with the opposing sides used by standard arguments. His early work concentrated on the relationship between propositions and the world. Later though, he repudiated much of his earlier work, maintaining that the meaning of words is best understood in their use, or, as he phrased it, within "the stream of life".

In his *Remarks on the Foundation of Mathematics* he denounced mathematical proofs as inferences and not descriptions of real properties in the world. For Wittgenstein, mathematics is a method of invention as opposed to discovery. His views here have since been largely either misinterpreted or rejected.

In the *Tractatus* Wittgenstein argues against philosophy as a cognitive discipline. According to his thinking here, there are no philosophical propositions or knowledge; if there were, they would be commonly accepted. Instead, philosophy has a different task—to clear away confusion. Philosophy should not hold theories; its role is to examine the rules that we use in words and grammar. And such rules are to be found in a clear and straightforward way; they do not contain hidden meanings. Philosophical problems stem from confusions over language and its use. For Wittgenstein, philosophy is a descriptive pursuit, clarifying concepts and dissolving problems; as such the role of philosophy is understanding and not knowledge.

Wittgenstein does not offer any metaphysical advance, but rather makes a significant "therapeutic" contribution to philosophy—helping us untangle many of the confusions that philosophy can so often and so readily deal out.

In our verses here Wittgenstein deliberately misunderstands Russell's words in order to point up the difference between his and Russell's view of how meaning is given to what is said.

Bertrand Russell and Ludwig Wittgenstein Take a Punt in the Stream of Life

The sun was shining on the Backs,
The Cam was smooth and still,
And those with punts who had the knacks
Went boating with a will.

Wittgenstein had never seen
How punting could be done,
But Russell saw that he was keen
To try to join the fun.

'Now, first we both must learn the ropes;'
Said Bert, 'I'll take the bow.'
Ludwig was young, Bertie had hopes
He'd learn to pole somehow.

So Wittgenstein stood by the punt
Awaiting Russell's bow,
But Russell meant, by bow, the front
Where he was sitting now.
'Where are the ropes,' asked Wittgenstein,
'That we have got to learn?'
'The painter's there, so we are fine;'
Said Bert, 'you take the stern.'

'Does he know how to punt, Bertie?
I'll be stern as I ought;
Will he be charging us a fee
Or something of that sort?'

'The stern's the rear', came back a sigh,
'The painter is a rope
That joins us to our berth, untie

The hitch if you can cope.'

Said Wittgenstein, 'I know my birth
Was privileged and rich

 But it strikes me with much mirth
To say there was *one* hitch.'

'The clove hitch is a sailor's knot;'
Said Bertie, 'set us loose,
Then take the pole, like it or not,
So you can be of use.'

'Why take a poll—we're only two;'
Said Ludwig, 'there is me
And if I'm not mistaken, you:
We surely can agree.'

'I'm really getting quite annoyed,'
Said Bertie, turning red;
'You misconstrue, dodge and avoid
Meaning in what I've said!

To move the punt you use a pole
Against the river bed;

I'd thought that that could be your role;
Let's go to moor instead.'

'Oh, G. E. Moore is coming too!'
Exclaimed young Wittgenstein;
'I'm sure he'll know just what to do,
He understands you fine.'

Now Russell said he'd had enough:
'There'll be no jaunt today;
With all my words you call my bluff,
I don't know what to say.'

Young Wittgenstein said, 'Take your ease,
I'll punt you where you will;
My words were only meant to tease,
And you have had your fill.

Your references to punting lore
Meant nothing much to me;
In fact I'd say they were a bore
And left me quite at sea.

You hold that trained minds like your own
Cut meaning like a knife;
But I think meaning's only shown
Within the stream of life.'

Jean Paul Sartre (1905-80)

Jean Paul Sartre, multi-talented philosopher and thinker, not only described the modern version of existentialism but excelled as a novelist, playwright, political theorist and literary critic.

At the beginning of the Second World War Sartre was conscripted into the French army, captured, released and then became involved in the French Resistance. After the war ended, even though he was sought after by universities, he turned aside from the academic life in favour of full time writing. Exploring and taking further the ideas of Kierkegaard and Heidegger, he produced philosophical works, plays and novels. He voiced political opinions on the public stage and became involved in what he recognised as a conflict between communism and Marxism. He turned down the offer of a Nobel Prize for Literature in 1964.

Sartre's contribution to philosophy is great indeed. Together with Camus he sits at the foundational heart of modern existentialism. His views captured in his novel concerning alienation, *Nausea*, and his major philosophical work *Being and Nothingness*, take further the underpinning of existentialism laid down by Kierkegaard and Heidegger and were a basis for this type of thinking until the late 1960s.

Sartre had a major impact on Western philosophy from the 1940s until the 1970s. Although since his death in 1980 his thinking has been superseded by post-structuralists such as Derrida and Deleuze, his influence cannot be ignored.

For all his intensity, his writing and commitment to the political stage, Sartre also had a lighter, more worldly side which allowed him to enjoy the fun that it can readily offer. The verses here take us on a trip which he makes with his long time lover Simone de Beauvoir to a fairground. The challenge to the reader is to discover the titles for his works amongst the entertainments and rides.

Jean Paul Sartre Goes to the Fair

In a city that's well known as our 'Gay Pari'
(The "s" isn't heard if you're French, as you see),
A philosopher lived not too far from Montmartre
And he went by the name of Monsieur Jean Paul Sartre.

His girlfriend Simone came to see him one day,
She said, 'Listen, Jean Paul, I've got something to say;
Enough of this work—you're in need of some sun,
The fair is in town, let's go and have fun!'

Jean Paul got his coat and then looked at his shoe,
'There's some iron in the sole, so that pair won't do;
I should do some work but I'll take a reprieve;
For the sake of my health we can lock up and leave.'

At the fair, Sartre tried at the coconut shy
To win a toy camera, but aimed just too high;

De Beauvoir took snaps, and laughed as she said,
'My shots are on target, you're in camera instead!'

The waltzer came next, but when he had seen
The violent motion, then Jean Paul turned green;
Nausea overtook him. He turned to Simone,
'I really can't face it, you ride it alone.'

While waiting, he watched children after their ride,
All dizzy and reeling from side to side;
'I'm glad I know better and now have attained
A ripe age of reason and so have refrained.'

To settle his stomach he was at a loss,
But Simone de Beauvoir bought candy floss.
It attracted the flies which wasn't ideal;
As a thing in itself it was only too real.

And then Gypsy Rose's tent came into view—
A respectable prostitute, soothsayer too—
'Let's see what she says that our future will hold;
It may be that fortune and fame is foretold.'

They entered the tent and sat down next to Rose
Who said, 'This is now what my crystal ball shows:
It's a picture of being where things are what they're not,
A nothingness, too, where they're not what you've got.'

Jean Paul was intrigued but Simone said, 'It's clear
We've got the idiot of the family right here;
This gypsy would pull the wool over our eyes,
Her claim to tell fortunes is just a disguise.'

They tried to get out, but the "No Exit" sign
Confused their attempt. The gypsy said, 'Fine.
You reject what I say, but I promise you'll see
That your own self-negation will alone set you free.'

They both stumbled out by the way they'd gone there,
Like men without shadows they now felt stripped bare.
'We went to the fair in good faith,' said Simone,
'But I think we had best leave the occult alone.'

'It's a valid idea,' said her boyfriend Jean Paul,
'That consciousness is the main clue to it all;
And what we create in our minds is the key;
It's the springboard for action which then makes us
free.

And what's more, a day that I thought would be lost
Has brought me a bonus, and that at no cost:
To go to the fair seemed temptation to shirk,
But it's given me titles for most of my work!'

Printed in Great Britain
by Amazon

80296559R10078